all you are

the
Gift

all you are

elizabeth karre

darbycreek
MINNEAPOLIS

Darby Creek
A division of Lerner Publishing Group, Inc.
241 First Avenue North
Minneapolis, MN 55401 USA

For reading levels and more information, look up this title at
www.lernerbooks.com.

Cover and interior photographs © Jitalia17/Vetta/Getty Images (basketball hoop); © iStockphoto.com/adventtr (circle logo); © iStockphoto.com/hh5800 (ribbon graphic).

Main body text set in Janson Text LT Std 12/17.5.
Typeface provided by Adobe Systems.

Library of Congress Cataloging-in-Publication Data

Karre, Elizabeth.
    All you are / by Elizabeth Karre.
        p.   cm. — (The gift)
    Summary: Da'Quan has never quite broken into the popular crowd at school, but when a strange dream-character gives him the ability to channel others' thoughts, Da'Quan is surprised by what he can learn from them.
    ISBN 978-1-4677-3510-0 (lib. bdg. : alk. paper)
    ISBN 978-1-4677-4644-1 (eBook)
    [1. Popularity—Fiction. 2. Magic—Fiction. 3. Empathy—Fiction. 4. Dating (Social customs)—Fiction. 5. Single-parent families—Fiction. 6. African Americans—Fiction.] I. Title.
PZ7.K1497All 2014
[Fic]—dc23   2013042948

Manufactured in the United States of America
1 – SB – 7/15/14

To everyone just trying to make it through

chapter one

It started when I walked into my room and this dude was in my bed.

"What the—?!" I yelled.

For a minute, looking at the back of his head on my pillow, I thought it was me. That was even more messed up than finding a random stranger in my room.

Then he slowly sat up, stretching and yawning. He was wearing my uncle's army T-shirt I always wear to bed. And my do-rag. And as he swung his legs out of the bed, I saw he had on my boxers too.

My heart was racing. I looked around my room for a weapon. I grabbed a textbook off my desk. But as I glanced at the book, I stopped short.

The words on the front were swimming. The letters were dancing around, sliding up and down the cover. I couldn't even really focus my eyes on any of them.

Sometimes I do have trouble reading. But I've learned how to step my way through words if I go slowly enough and try to stay cool. This was something else. This meant something good.

I laughed out loud and spun around to the guy. He was just sitting on the bed, watching me. I could see now—now that I knew he wasn't a threat—that he didn't look much like me. Lighter skin, kind of short. A little girly. Maybe it was his superlong eyelashes.

"See you later, man," I said as I ran over to the window. I yanked it open.

"What are you going to do?" he asked.

"Fly," I said. "Maybe beat up Montez. And find Ashantay."

Ashantay naked. Naked Ashantay, I thought over and over. Or maybe in something sexy. Bikini? Short skirt, no underwear? Sometimes I got overwhelmed by the possibilities.

The dude snorted. "In your dreams, man."

"Yeah, exactly," I said. "This *is* a dream, and I'm controlling it." I had one leg out the window.

Dude raised his eyebrows. "How do you know it's a dream?" he asked.

"This," I said, holding up the book and pointing at the words. "Moving words, it's my cue. But once you know—" I pointed at the giant flowers bursting out of the wall, growing and shrinking. They looked just like the ones I got for Mom's birthday. "You see that everything's just crazy dream stuff." Then I pointed at him.

"Me?" he said, acting all surprised. "You think I'm just a dream? What do you know about dreaming anyway?"

"I know how to lucid dream," I said proudly. I couldn't wait to explain it to him. Which is weird because I'd never talked about it with anyone. It was my secret. It made me special.

He raised his eyebrows again. "Very impressive. How did you learn?"

"My middle school science teacher told us about it. He said you could learn to wake up in your dream and control it. If it was a bad dream, you could stop the punk from coming at you, turn him into something else. You could make good stuff happen too, whatever you want. Sounded awesome to me. I used to have a lot of nightmares."

"But how did you learn to do it?" Dude asked, scratching his chest.

"I asked him later. He said if you wrote down your dreams after you woke up, you could start to look for the things that happened only in dreams. One of the signs is words moving, and that always happened to me. Used to be part of my nightmares about not being able to read. Anyway, once you learn your signs, you can start to know when you're dreaming. Takes a lot of practice before you don't wake yourself all the way up, but I got it down now."

I turned back to the window. I was ready to take off.

"So what else do you do in your dreams besides the three Fs? Fly, fight, ... ya know," he smiled.

I shrugged. Maybe that was another reason why I didn't talk about lucid dreaming with anyone.

Suddenly the dude was there behind me, his hand on my shoulder.

"Well, that's a gift, lucid dreaming. But I think you're ready for something you can use when you're actually awake."

chapter two

"Would you like a gift?" Dude asked me, his hand still on my shoulder.

I shrugged him off and jumped out of the window.

Next thing I knew, I was back in my room with the window closed. I looked around hopefully for Ashantay, but there was just that guy.

I closed my eyes and tried to picture Ashantay. When I opened them, the dude was just smiling at me.

"Da'Quan, what do you want most?" he asked, leaning close to me.

Hey, I knew I was dreaming and sometimes dreams helped me figure things out. So why not be honest?

"To be in with them," I said.

"Them?" he asked.

"Montez. Iesha. And them," I said, frustrated. How to explain? It wasn't always the same people, but you knew who they were. The people having the best time at lunch, who had the best parties. The prettiest girls. The best athletes. Them.

"Okaaaay," he said, tipping his head. "And 'to be in' means . . . ?"

I was getting impatient. I could wake up any minute, and I hadn't gotten laid yet. "You know, I wouldn't have to wonder if it's okay if I sit with them at lunch or if I'll be invited to something. Everyone would laugh at my jokes. I could date any of the girls, like Ashantay. But I gotta go, Okay, man?"

The dude thrust a book at me. "Take a look in there, and see if there's anything that might help you."

I was surprised the words on the book weren't jumping around. GIFTS, it said on the cover. It fell open as I took it.

Invisibility

Mind reading

Truth detection

Gender switching

"What is this?" I asked, suspicious.

"Like it says, a list of gifts I could give you. But you only get one," the guy said.

"What are you, some kind of black guy fairy godmother?" I said, getting smart.

He just looked at me.

"Oh my God, you are!" I said. "Or are you more like the genie in Aladdin? Except not as good 'cause you can only give me one wish instead of three." I was busting up laughing now.

The dude grabbed the book from me, flipping through the pages. "You know what I like for you," he said, giving me a once-over look, the kind my mom's friends do when they are deciding if an outfit is good or not. "I like channeling for you."

"What's that?" I asked.

He slammed the book closed, and it disappeared. "Sounds like you envy them, whoever they are. You want to be *them*. You want to have what they have. Channeling can let you do that."

"Man, you are cra-zay," I said.

"Okay, if you're not interested—" the dude said and started to climb back into my bed and pull up the covers.

"Whoa, just chill out," I said. "I'll listen if you want to tell me more."

"If *I* want?" the dude said. "*Me?* This is about *you*, Da'Quan. And you want a lot. But I guess you don't want it enough. Or maybe you think you have what it takes all on your own. Well, good luck, brother."

I was frozen by his words. Actually, even though I tried to stay positive like my mom always said, I knew I didn't have what it took; otherwise, I'd already be in. I'd been hanging out around the edges of that group for years. Since middle school. And I still couldn't really say I was friends with any of them.

I was hoping this year would be different, but really, why would it be? I was still average.

Okay at sports, funny once in a while, not ugly but not a chick magnet . . . The only person who thought I was something special was my mom, and that's just a mom's job.

"Okay," I said, my voice thick. "I need help. So tell me about this channeling thing."

chapter three

When I woke up, I was holding my radio. The cord was stretched so tight that the plug was starting to pull out of the outlet. The radio was still faintly buzzing, though, half tuned in to the jazz station where my cousin works. I could hear the morning DJ, Unique, over the sound of static.

I slapped the radio to shut it up, put it on the nightstand, and fell back on my bed. I closed my eyes trying to remember what the dude had said about my new magical power. Something about it being like finding a radio station.

Channeling lets you share a trait someone else has.

Wait, what? What do you mean, a trait?

Traits make people what they are. Like, some of your mom's traits are that she's hard working, impatient, impulsive, affectionate, and bossy.

Okaaaay . . . So?

Once you have the gift of channeling, you're like—like the antenna on your radio. You can tune into the station of someone's trait, and it will play in you.

This is so messed up. First, you're talking about channels, like TV, and now you're talking about radios. And I don't see no antenna on my radio.

Then the dude tried to explain how radios and TVs work, and I hated him because he was making me feel stupid. I shook my head. I didn't need to remember that. But the next part—

I'll just show you. Say you wanted to channel my trait of extreme intelligence. He smirked. I had to stop myself from smashing his face. *You can— you just have to tune into it.*

But . . . how?

Just try; you have the power now. It helps to relax, so you might want to stop clenching your fists.

And then I was doing it; don't ask me how. It felt like something new flowing through me. I looked at my radio, and I could swear I saw the invisible radio waves he was going on about before. If I had taken the back off the radio, I could have told you what each part was inside. It all made perfect sense.

But—

A few warnings. He held up a hand. *I've heard from other channelers that it's best to tune in to someone's essence, their most important trait. The trait that defines them.*

How—

I don't have a lot of experience with channeling, probably because I've got it all already. He smirked again. *So you'll have to figure it out for yourself. But I know at least this one girl said it wasn't working the way she thought it would. Something about getting traits she wasn't expecting. Oh, and I'm not sure how long it lasts, either. Do you still feel smart?*

I might have hit him then; things got fuzzy after that.

I stretched and yawned. It was Sunday. Mom would want me to go to church with her. And school started on Tuesday.

chapter four

After church (where Mom made me go up front for a special prayer for a good school year for all the kids), I drifted over to the park to shoot some hoops or hang out if some of the guys showed up. A couple of times this summer I had found out about a party that way.

Daniel was there shooting threes. We started playing one-on-one, but it was dumb because he was whuping me bad. Like I said, I'm average. I was on the freshman team last year. Daniel was definitely going to make varsity this year as a sophomore. I hadn't decided if I even wanted to try out again this year.

Daniel was pretty nice so he didn't say anything, but you could tell he just couldn't hold himself back. He just kept driving by me. We weren't even really keeping score because it was pointless. But I guess it was better than if he had held back, like I was some little kid he was trying to let win.

When Montez and the other guys showed up, Daniel looked pretty relieved. Montez made teams (he didn't take me) and three guys on my team just moved onto the court, so I sat down.

I tried cheering for my boys. But after a while, when none of them were coming out so I could go in, I just sat. That hot feeling was building up in me again. The dude had called it *envy* or *wanting*. But who wouldn't want to play like Daniel? It was better than being ignored, sitting on the bench like somebody's little brother.

Just when I was wondering if anybody would even notice if I went home, I remembered the rest of my dream. A magic power would be useful right now, I thought sourly.

I watched a guy walking a dog across the park. It was a poodle, looking exactly like in a cartoon. What a stupid dog. The guy and the poodle both looked at me. It looked kind of like the dude in my dream. Then he winked at me and disappeared behind a tree.

I shook my head and closed my eyes. Suddenly Daniel's voice sounded louder than everyone else's even though he was across the court. I reached out with my mind—

Forget it, I can't describe what it felt like. It just sounds stupid and sci-fi. Best I can say is that I knew where he was even though I had my eyes closed, and I could feel things, energies and junk like that—things that the TV psychics talk about. But then I hesitated.

The dude had said something about finding someone's strongest trait thing. Tuning in to Daniel was actually like hearing a bunch of different music playing at once. I mean, obviously the guy had more going on in him than crazy basketball skills.

But wasn't basketball what people knew about Daniel? I was sure it was why he was in with Montez and them. He never trash-talked Montez, but everyone knew Daniel had better game. He was pretty quiet on and off the court. He wasn't a supergood student as far as I knew. Except for watching him play, he was kind of boring, I thought.

Whatever, I thought and took a deep breath. *Basketball is what I want.* And so I channeled it.

chapter five

Someone's phone going off made me open my eyes.

"C'mon, man!" Montez yelled in frustration. He threw the ball at Daniel's back as Daniel jogged off the court to his stuff. "I swear Shaquetta won't stop putting out even if you don't answer every single one of her frickin' calls!"

The game stopped while Daniel talked to Shaquetta. The guys were all grumbling or making jokes about Shaquetta and Daniel.

I had forgotten about Shaquetta. She and Daniel had been going together since eighth grade. They walked together to every class and stood right next to the door making out before they said good-bye. Everybody had gotten so used to it, nobody even noticed them lip-locked anymore. I wondered why she wasn't there—she usually came to watch Daniel even if he was just playing with the guys.

I wondered if my channeling had worked. Maybe I'd just go to the next park by myself and see if I could try some of Daniel's moves. I stood up and stretched.

"Hey, Da'Quan, get out here," Montez yelled. "We're not waiting all day for *Danielle* to suck up to his girlfriend."

Trying not to look too excited, I pulled off my shirt, strolled onto the court, and nodded that I was ready.

In the beginning, that game was the best. With Daniel's skills flowing through me, it wasn't just that I could jump higher, run faster, shoot better. No, his secret, I discovered, was how he could see the whole game at once. Just like he was sitting up on the hoop, watching everything in slow motion. I felt like I always knew exactly where the ball was going to be. I was so hot.

I also loved how pissed off it made Montez. I could tell when he called me into the game, he thought it gave him a chance to beat on Daniel's team. But not this time.

Pretty soon Montez was playing dirty, throwing elbows and trying to hold me. The rest of his team started doing it too. At first I didn't care so much because I was so good it was barely slowing me down. But then I took an elbow to the mouth and it hurt.

"What the—?!" I yelled, holding my mouth.

"Oops, did you get hurt, Quany?" Montez mocked. "Maybe you're not as good as you thought."

I couldn't believe he was challenging my skills. Without thinking, I shoved him.

Montez's eyes lit up with rage. I'll admit it, usually I was kind of scared of him. But not now. And for some reason, he didn't immediately start beating on me like I expected.

"What'd you do that for?" he yelled. "Terrell's the one who hit you, crybaby."

Most of the time I don't like fights, probably because I lose more than I win. But today I didn't care. I had to prove I wasn't going to take that disrespect. Then I was going to whup everyone in basketball to prove I was the best. At least that was what I was thinking.

The fight didn't last long before the guys broke it up. I got some good hits in on Montez, though. And on Terrell too, as he tried to push us apart, just in case it was Terrell whose elbow hit my mouth by the basket.

While Montez and me were being held apart, Rashawn stepped into the middle.

"C'mon, y'all, I came here to play ball and y'all are messing up a good game. If you can't chill out, you'd better sit out or go fight somewhere else, but we gonna keep playing," he said.

I had to smile, his tone was just like someone's mama when her kids are fighting.

"I'm cool," I said, wiping the blood on my

face with my hand and wiping it on my shorts. My team's hands loosened, and they patted my back.

Montez just grunted, but everyone knew that was the best they'd get from him, so they let him go.

While Daniel was still on the phone with his back to us and then while he sat on the bench watching, I not only held the lead, I increased it. Montez got so pissed that he said this was all crap and he wanted to eat lunch.

As I rubbed my sweaty face with my shirt, Daniel put his hand on my shoulder.

"You were on fire, man," he said. "Thanks for stepping in for me."

I couldn't stop smiling. "No," I said. "Thank *you*."

He looked confused. "What for?"

"For letting me play." I almost giggled.

He looked embarrassed. "Uhh, I mean—Shaquetta—"

Shaking my head, I slapped him on the back and went to high-five with some of the guys. He so did not know what I was talking about.

chapter six

But then that night, having dinner with my mom, I started having this strange feeling. Usually with my family I feel relaxed. I know they love me no matter what—I hadn't ever questioned that before. That's just what family is. If you're a freak, in a bad mood, looking ugly, they still got you. As long as you're not hurting anybody, of course.

I was kind of bragging about the game to my mom. Because she's my mom, I can do that. But

I felt like she wasn't listening.

"How can you be proud of me if you ain't listening to me telling you about how good I played?" I whined. I sounded like my little cousin when she wants something.

"Sorry, baby, I'm just distracted. Thinkin' about money again. I got to make a susu payment on Friday. Don't go to the store before Friday so I can see how much money I got. There's plenty of food, just maybe not your favorites right now," Mom said.

"When is it your turn for the susu money?" I asked.

Mom counted on her fingers. "Friday's Tiffany, then two weeks and it's Sunshine, then two weeks is Jamilla, and then it's me. Seven weeks. Mmm, can't wait."

"Can I get a new phone?" I asked. I didn't like people to see my phone; it was embarrassing.

"No, boy, you know that money's for us to do something nice together—go someplace. You got some days off school then—that's why I picked that payday to get the susu money."

I pouted. "Feels like you don't care about me."

She stared at me. "Did you get too much sun today or something? You've never tried that one on me before; I thought because you knew that's the biggest lie there is.

"And what's this about me needing to hear about how good you played some game to be proud of you? Da'Quan, I'm happy to hear your stories and I'm happy if you liked how you played, but I thought you had it figured out by now that I'm proud of you just because you're my son. Nothing can change my love for you."

I got choked up and had to look at my plate. But instead of feeling good like I usually did when my mom said she loved me, a voice in my head said, *She's just saying that because she thinks she has to.*

I almost whipped my head around. Where did that come from?

It only got worse when my uncle and cousin stopped by later.

Usually I loved hanging out with them. I really didn't mind that it was just me and my mom, but it was always good to be with the men in my family. My cousin Shaun is one of the nicest guys. That's probably why no one ever gives him hassle, least that I know about. I mean, the guy worked at a jazz radio station—how weird is that? People always thought it was awesome my cousin was a DJ until they found out about the music.

Most people in my family were so comfortable just being who they were. I think that's why I always felt so relaxed with them. They were them; I was me—whoever that was—and that was all fine.

I guess that's why I wanted to be friends with the right people at school. I thought I could get that comfortable feeling at school too if I was so popular no one would question what I did or said. I'm sure Montez could cry after a game and no one would say anything—he was that on top.

Maybe if Shaun had been closer to my age and we'd gone to school together, like so many cousins I knew, I wouldn't have been looking so hard to get in so I could feel untouchable.

But that night I couldn't find that feeling even with Shaun, my uncle, and my mom. When Shaun teased me gently about my music,

I got really anxious and mad.

"It doesn't make me stupid to like what I like," I snarled. "You're the freak, Shaun. I just listen to what everyone listens to."

Mom looked surprised I'd be like that with Shaun.

But Shaun just nodded and smiled. "No doubt, Quan, you're in the mainstream and I'm not. I just like keeping our heritage alive. Hey, do you still want to see the station? I asked and I can give you a tour."

"Yeah," I muttered, feeling bad.

"It's not much to see—just a few crowded rooms. But I know I promised you," Shaun said.

"So it's just because you promised?" I blurted out.

Shaun and everyone else looked confused. "Yeah, don't you remember when I said I'd try to get you in to see behind the scenes?" he asked.

"Never mind," I said. *He doesn't really want to be with you*, the voice said. *He just feels he has to keep his promise. Probably his dad is making him.*

It went on that way all night.

When my uncle said, "Last day of summer

tomorrow, huh? You looking forward to school, Quan?" The voice in my head said, *He thinks you still can't read and because you're stupid, you must hate school. And he knows you have no friends.*

It made it hard to talk to everyone with that voice telling me all those bad things. I didn't completely believe it—this was my family, and they were just saying regular things, enjoying hanging out together like usual.

I was thinking about just going into my room when Shaun asked if I wanted to shoot hoops. Remembering the game, I smiled for the first time that night.

My uncle came too, and we played. I made every single shot except one right at the end. That put me back in a bad mood.

"Whoa, Quan, you're in the flow," my uncle said, slapping me on the back.

The only nice thing he can say about you is about something that ain't yours, said the voice. It made everything suck.

We walked back home in silence.

chapter seven

There's nothing to do on Labor Day so I went back to the park. If basketball was the one thing I was good at now, I should do it, I thought.

Daniel was there again with Shaquetta watching him this time. There seemed to be something weird with them. *It's because you're here,* the voice said. *They were just talking about you.*

Daniel and I played for a while. I was still good, but I started making mistakes again. Even though I was just playing with one other person,

I didn't have that feeling anymore like I knew exactly what was going to happen. I couldn't see the court from above anymore.

When the other guys came, I was ready to sit out. It felt like the skills I had channeled from Daniel were flowing out of me. After yesterday, I didn't want anyone seeing how I was playing like myself again. When Montez wanted me on his team, I said I would go in later. He thought I was still mad from the fight.

I sat down the bench from Shaquetta. After a while she looked up from her phone.

"Let me ask you a question, Da'Quan," she said. She looked kind of angry. "How is it that a person can have everything and still be so insecure?"

This seemed like one of those dumb questions girls asked that no one could answer. I shrugged.

"You're helpful," she snapped.

"I don't know what you're talking about," I said. "Who's insecure?"

"Daniel," she said, watching him make a free throw. "He just can't take yes for an answer.

He never feels good enough. He's got to prove himself over and over, and I'm tired of it; I really am. Have you seen how mad he gets when he thinks he's being disrespected?"

Her face looked sad, but this was a lot more information than I thought I wanted. I had never paid Daniel and Shaquetta much attention. They were in but on the edges. Probably because they were so tied up with each other. Also, if I thought about what got them in, it was Daniel and basketball and Shaquetta . . .

I studied her for a moment. She was pretty tight with Ashantay and sometimes was all BFF with Iesha too. Maybe it was her clothes. But not just that, she was always looking perfect. "Put together" my mom called it. But I didn't think Shaquetta wore really expensive stuff like Iesha; she just knew how to make anything look good.

I looked at my clothes. That was something I could use help with. I didn't know what to wear tomorrow on the first day of school. I had been thinking of buying something today; I just didn't know what. I had some money. I wished I had a girlfriend to take me shopping.

Suddenly I knew what to do.

"Hey, Shaquetta," I said. "How you always know what to wear?"

She got a slow smile. "I just always have. I look at what other people wear. I look at what they got up in the windows at the mall. I know what looks good on me. And I know what doesn't look good on other people . . . but they don't always want to hear it." She said that last part so quiet that I almost didn't hear it. I didn't know what she meant anyway.

She turned back to her phone. I closed my eyes and tuned in. This time, it was even easier to pick out what I wanted. There were some other things there inside Shaquetta that looked a little scary. Whatever—I needed some fashion sense, and so I took it.

chapter eight

When I opened my eyes, I could see exactly why everything about Shaquetta worked so well together. Even how the color of her hair played off the color of her bag. Usually I barely noticed girls' bags except when I tripped over them in class.

"I like your hair, Shaquetta," I couldn't help myself saying.

"Cost enough, it better look good," Shaquetta snapped not looking up.

I laughed. "That's what my mom always says too. But you change your hair a lot, don't you?"

Shaquetta gave me a weird look. "Worry about you instead, Da'Quan. Have you changed anything about yourself since eighth grade? I swear, you've been wearing that same crap T-shirt for years."

I laughed again. "You are so right. I'm going shopping today."

"Well, good luck," she muttered.

"Where you going?" Terrell asked, standing right next to me. I hadn't noticed the game broke up.

"The mall," I said.

Terrell hesitated. "I gotta go to the mall too. If you want . . ."

"Sure," I said, flattered he wanted to hang out with me. He was Montez's best boy most of the time. Guess that one good basketball game made me cooler than I realized. Or maybe the fight. "Yeah, you could use new clothes," I said before I could stop myself. It was true, but why did I say it?

Terrell looked surprised and a little annoyed.

"I just gotta stop at home and get my cash," I said quickly.

"Yeah, I gotta get my little sister," he said. "My mom said I have to take her to get a new backpack. Hers got stolen last year."

So that was why he wanted to hang with me—I was better than his sister.

We agreed to meet at the bus stop.

When Terrell walked up with his sister, I couldn't stop staring at her.

"Did your mom use kiddie perm on your hair?" I said. It was not pretty.

She nodded, miserably. "Yeah, it hurt and now it looks bad."

"You gotta get that fixed," I said. "It looks *real* bad."

She burst into tears. Terrell gave me a dirty look.

"Man, just shut up and leave her alone. My mom don't have the money to take her to get her hair done. She fixed it; it's not that bad."

"I want my hair fixed *for real* instead of a new backpack," Terrell's sister wailed.

"Shut up," Terrell said, pushing her up the

steps of the bus. "You gotta have a backpack for school."

On the bus there were exactly two people who looked good. That surprised me because usually most girls looked good to me, especially in the summer when they were wearing short shorts and tank tops. But now a lot of those girls just looked tacky. Didn't they know how to show it off the right way?

At the mall I couldn't wait to start shopping. I wouldn't let Terrell go in some of the stores he wanted.

"That stuff's all wrong for you," I said.

"What are you talking about?" he said, staring at me. I just walked on, and his sister followed me. I noticed she had on good shoes for her outfit, and I told her so.

She beamed. "I picked them out for new school shoes."

Me and Terrell's sister had a great time. She was really good at finding stuff on sale that was still classic. She tried to help Terrell, but he told her to get lost. Then he left for the food court.

Finally, I had something great to wear

tomorrow. It was different than anything I'd worn before, but I thought I looked amazing in it. After I paid, I gave the money I still had left to Terrell's little sister.

"Here," I said. "You can start saving for new hair. Thanks for your help."

"A weave," she breathed. "Think my mom would let me?"

"Or next time," I said, "just leave it alone and spend the money on more shoes."

She looked hard at me. "Do you like girls with natural hair?"

I shrugged. Did I know any girls with natural hair? I wondered when all the girls' hair had changed. I guess in elementary school I was too busy with the guys to notice. I had real friends then, and I wasn't worrying yet about being in or about girls.

When we found Terrell, he looked pretty mad.

"We got to get your backpack and go," he said to his sister, barely looking at me.

"I got an idea about that," I said.

chapter nine

Terrell tried to shoot down my idea, but since his sister was going with me, he had to come. When we stood up to get off the bus at the Goodwill, he grabbed his sister's arm.

"C'mon, there's a Target in a few more blocks. You don't want none of them nasty bags they got at Goodwill. Everyone at school will laugh at you."

She just pulled away and followed me.

Just like I hoped, there were some options at

Goodwill. At first she picked a turquoise leather bag with two little handles. But then Terrell screamed that she had to be able to fit a folder and a book in it.

I agreed that was a good idea even though the bag was supercute.

The one she finally picked was lime green with one long strap she could put over her shoulder. Terrell said no, it was too big and she'd never be able to carry it. So I showed them how she could wear it with the strap across her chest and the bag on her hip. Best of all, it was only three bucks.

"Give me all the money Mom gave you for my backpack," she said to Terrell as we were waiting in line. He wasn't talking anymore. He just handed it over and went to sit at the bus stop.

"Now I got twenty-six dollars," Terrell's sister said as we went out. "I don't know if that's enough for my hair."

"You're little and cute—you should be able to charm somebody into doing something. Hey, go to the place my mom goes. Shirley, who owns it—she runs my mom's susu, and she's really nice. She used to cut my hair for free when I was little, before I could go to the barbershop by myself."

Terrell's sister threw her arms around me. "I love you," she said as the bus pulled up. Terrell got on without looking at us.

Just as the bus was pulling away, somebody pounded on the door. When he came down the aisle, I saw it was Tommy Her. He was practically bald.

"Man, what happened to you?" I asked, shocked. "Leave that look to the black brothers. You just look like a thug."

Tommy seemed surprised, but he laughed. "Hey, Da'Quan, good to see you too. Yeah, my dad came home with clippers yesterday and said my hair had got too long over the summer. But I didn't know until he started how bad it was going to be. I think he was going for the Buddhist monk look for me."

He ran his hand over his head and made a face.

I felt bad. I shouldn't have said anything. In

fact, I couldn't believe I had. I never would have said anything like that before to anyone, and I actually liked Tommy.

"Does your hair grow fast?" I asked, trying to make him feel better. "Pretty soon you'll have that pointy swoop thing you Asian guys do with your front hair back again."

Tommy almost fell over laughing. "You mean the gel in the bangs? Yeah, someday. Unless I decide to be a monk." He slapped my hand and headed to the back of the bus where a bunch of Asian guys were sitting.

"Oh my God," Terrell said through his teeth. "Are you gay or something? What is wrong with you?"

"You don't like Tommy?" I asked.

"I know I'm not getting turned on by the gel in his hair," Terrell said rolling his eyes. "Or wasting all day buying crap with girls."

"Just ignore him," said his sister. "He's jealous he don't got no taste."

The rest of the ride home I wondered about these things I was saying. First, I was having opinions about stuff I'd never cared about before. Then I couldn't keep them to myself like I usually did with a lot of stuff I thought. Maybe it was just part of what I'd channeled from Shaquetta.

But on the good side, I wasn't hearing that awful voice in my head anymore. The one that kept tearing me down, making me feel like I wasn't ever in. Telling me that I always had to prove myself worthy, even to my family.

Maybe that voice had come from Daniel—it left with the basketball skills. But, man, that was hard to believe. I had no idea why Daniel would feel that way. Things seemed pretty good with him to me—hot girlfriend, top skills, in with them since the first time anyone saw him play. What else could he want?

chapter ten

It was good that Mom worked late that night, getting holiday overtime. The more I thought about her clothes, the more I could see what was wrong with a lot of them. But did she want to hear that? When she had money, she loved to go shopping with Aunty Z. So she must have thought her stuff looked good.

She got home right as I was getting ready for bed.

"You got your hair done," I blurted out.

Then I pinched my leg to remind myself not to say anything else. I thought it was really ugly.

"I can't believe you noticed," she said, surprised. "How was your day, baby? Are you ready for school tomorrow?"

"Yeah, I got some clothes for tomorrow," I said proudly, showing them to her.

She raised her eyebrows. "Those are some nice threads, Da'Quan. A little different than your usual, though, huh? They look expensive."

I told her what I paid, and she nodded approvingly. My mom loves a deal.

"I guess I should take you with me next time I go shopping. But I wasn't just talking about clothes. I mean is your *brain* ready to work. Because I want to see you work this year, Quan. You know it's important you do well in school. You gonna do the math team this year?"

"God, Mom, no! I mean, I don't think I'll have time. But I promise I'll get good grades," I said quickly as she opened her mouth. "So how you like your new hair?" I said to change the subject. Then I pinched my leg again. I shouldn't go there.

She cut her eyes at me to show me she knew what I was doing. Then she ran her hand carefully over her hair and sighed.

"I don't think it's right for me. What you think, baby? Give me the male perspective," she teased.

I paused. "I liked it better before," I said carefully.

"Okay, next time you coming with me to get my hair done and buy me new clothes. Mother-son bonding time." She giggled and gave me a hug. "Night-night, baby. I love you. Sleep good and get that brain ready." She pretended to knock on my head.

As I lay in bed, I thought about what I wanted this school year. I wanted it to be different than last year. I definitely didn't want it to be like middle school.

I couldn't believe my mom had asked about math team. I hadn't done that since seventh grade. And I only did it because my best friend from elementary school, James, did it. I did like math, but I wasn't as good at it as he was.

But then I realized how dumb everyone else

thought it was so I quit before the big competition. And I pretty much stopped hanging out with James. In eighth grade we barely talked. And last year he went to some math and science charter school. Sometimes I still saw him in the neighborhood, but he usually acted like he didn't know me.

James was the last real friend I had. That thought made me sad. I squeezed my pillow and tried to push it away. But I couldn't stop my mind from going over the last two years.

I hung around the edges of Montez and Iesha's crowd, trying not to look pathetic, trying to figure out what I needed to get in. Sometimes I did sit with them at lunch. I even got invited to a few parties. And I had even made out with some of the girls—none of that never went nowhere so I tried to pretend like I was a player.

But this year will be different, I tried to tell myself. I still wasn't sure if this channeling "gift" was something real. But lying in the dark, it seemed believable. I felt different each time I thought I'd done it. I'd done things I couldn't do before. So that was going to help me this year. Whatever I needed to be cool, I could just take it from someone else, and no one would ever know. I could be the best at everything if I wanted.

But I had to be a little more careful, I decided. I thought I was getting other stuff besides what I wanted. I should try to find out what bad stuff was inside people before I channeled from them. And the dude had said something about people's essences. Maybe if I tried to channel what was someone's essence, I wouldn't get their crap too.

Now I had that good sleepy feeling, like I was sinking into the softest bed. This year I was going to get invited to Iesha's homecoming party. And date Ashantay. And then I'd really be in with them.

Anything was possible.

chapter eleven

When I got dressed in the morning, I wasn't so sure about my clothes anymore. I'd never worn anything like that before. *Don't be a wimp*, I told myself.

"You should get a new bathrobe," I told my mom while I ate a Pop-Tart and she drank coffee with her eyes closed. "That color makes your skin look bad."

She opened her eyes and squinted at me. "Then I guess it's a good thing you the only one gotta look at this ugly old lady in the morning."

"I mean, I'm just saying. You don't hafta get mad."

"Da'Quan, don't you have somewhere to be?" she asked all smart. "Have a good day at school, and I'll see you later. If you lucky, I won't be wearing this."

Cussing to myself, I slammed out the door.

When Shaquetta came into my homeroom, she stopped dead.

"Oh my GOD, Da'Quan. What are you wearing?" she said super loud.

"Shut up," I told her. I was not in the mood. Every minute my clothes were seeming stupider and stupider. And I'd seen Ashantay's name on the homeroom list. I didn't want Shaquetta making fun of me in front of Ashantay.

"No, no, I like it. It's bold. It's got vision. I just can't believe you're wearing it. You usually wear such boring stuff, like so many of the guys around here. Okay, tell me, who picked it out for you?" Shaquetta demanded.

I started to smile. "A girl with good fashion sense," I said. "She's a lot like you."

"Wha-at? Boy, you just playing me. You got some girlfriend I don't know about?"

I just smiled mysteriously. Then my smile got even bigger and I blushed because Ashantay had walked in.

Shaquetta grabbed Ashantay. "Look at Da'Quan. He said some chick helped him pick out his clothes. Who you think it is?"

Ashantay smiled at me. She was so nice. She always had been. "Looks good, Da'Quan. I like that color green, see?" She held up her purse. It was the same color.

"Ooooh, is there something I should know?" Shaquetta said. "You guys all matchy, you goin' shoppin', you havin' babies together—mmmm, mmm!" She busted out laughing.

Ashantay rolled her eyes. "Shut up, Shaquetta." But she was smiling like she didn't mind being teased about me. I had to look at my desk I was so bubbly feeling inside. Maybe this was going to work out for real.

When I walked into first lunch, I scanned the room as I got in line. I hated this part of school starting—trying to figure out who I could sit with, getting in with the right table.

"Mmm, it's Ashantay's new man gettin' himself some pizza," I heard Shaquetta say behind me. "Daniel, why don't you ever get clothes like that when we go shopping?" she said.

I couldn't hear what Daniel said, but I heard Shaquetta's irritated sound. "Just because I like Da'Quan's clothes don't mean I don't love you," she said. "Stop being stupid."

"Here we go again," said someone else behind me as I left the line. I turned and saw Ashantay. My heart jumped.

"You have this lunch?" I said, stupidly.

She held up her tray. "Yeah."

"What do you mean, 'Here we go'...?" I asked.

"Umm, could we sit down somewhere?" Ashantay said. I followed her over by the window. I kinda looked around for Montez or the other guys in case they already had a table, but mostly I looked at her butt. It was a fine butt, and I wanted to go where it was going.

chapter twelve

"Haven't you noticed how much Shaquetta and Daniel are fighting?" Ashantay said, whipping her ketchup packet back and forth.

"But they've been going together forever," I said, trying not to talk with food in my mouth. "Maybe Shaquetta shouldn't keep telling Daniel what's wrong with him. Guys don't like that."

"Well, I don't think anybody likes it, but that's just Shaquetta, you know?" Ashantay said. "She's always had trouble keeping her opinions to herself, especially if it's about how somebody looks. And she's usually right. She does have good taste."

"But it's extra hard for Daniel," I said, leaning across the table. "He's kind of . . . insecure inside."

Ashantay studied me. "I didn't know you knew him so well."

I shrugged as Shaquetta and Daniel sat down with us, both looking mad. Montez was right behind them, and pretty soon the table filled up. Even though I was sitting mostly in the middle, everyone's attention was focused on Montez's end.

I started feeling on the edges, like always. Ashantay wasn't talking anymore so that wasn't helping. I didn't think Montez was still mad from the fight, but it was hard to tell. Montez hadn't never liked me much, I thought, picking at my lunch. That was part of my problem with everyone since they followed Montez.

Terrell said something. Montez doubled over laughing, Terrell leaning on him. Maybe I needed what Terrell had. He had been tight with Montez since middle school. I wondered what Montez liked best about Terrell. It wasn't something I could ask him; that would be stupid.

"Pretty stupid," Ashantay said, like she could read my thoughts. But then I saw she was pointing at Montez and Terrell with her french fry.

"Huh?" I said.

"I thought you was listening; you were staring right at them. They just thinking they're soooo funny, making fun of that girl over there." She jerked her head to the side.

I looked over at the other table. It was a bunch of average-looking girls.

"Why do you think Montez likes Terrell?" I blurted out.

Ashantay raised her eyebrows. "Probably because Terrell does whatever Montez tells him, laughs at his jokes, that junk. Montez didn't always used to be such an a-hole. We went together in sixth grade." She smiled.

"Huh," I said sourly. I pushed that thought away. "Maybe it's because he's funny. Terrell can make everybody laugh when he wants to."

Ashantay shrugged. "He was funny back in

third grade when he talked like different cartoon characters. But now that all he does is talk about how ugly some girl is or how gay some guy seems, he hasn't made me laugh in a long time."

"It's gotta be something," I said to myself as the bell rang.

chapter thirteen

By the end of the week, everything felt just like last year. I had totally lost whatever I got from Shaquetta and couldn't see how to make my clothes interesting. It didn't matter where at the lunch table I sat, the action was always somewhere else. And Ashantay was still being nice, but she spent a lot of time talking to Shaquetta.

I needed to do something. Homecoming was only a few weeks away. I had to find a way to ask Ashantay to the dance and get invited to

Iesha's party. I was not going to let this year be like last year.

Who had something I could channel but wouldn't give me something bad at the same time? I definitely couldn't handle that voice from Daniel. Shaquetta hadn't been too bad. But I didn't think understanding fashion would give me enough of a leg up.

I kept coming back to Terrell. He never had to worry that he'd get to sit at the lunch table. If he came in late and there wasn't space, Montez would make somebody move to the next table. Sometimes me.

And Terrell was definitely going to Iesha's party, no question—they had been going together since the beginning of the school year. But I didn't know if Ashantay would go to the dance with someone like Terrell.

Now, I know what you're thinking. Why not channel that certain something from Montez? After all, he was the man on top. The truth is, I was scared. When Montez was angry, he was . . . It's hard to explain. Like he went kind of crazy. I wasn't sure I wanted any part of him inside me.

And I didn't know why he was on top and had been since everyone met in middle school. Maybe because everyone else was scared of him too. And did Montez have anything that would help me with Ashantay?

No, I told myself, Montez was a bad idea. Whatever he had there was only room for one person like him. If he thought I was challenging him, who knew what he would do? I just wanted to be in, be so tight and secure with them that I didn't have to worry. I didn't have to be on top.

But before I tried to channel anything from Terrell, I wanted to know more about him. I decided to catch him after school. Like me, he wasn't on the football team—that had to mean he had something special, I thought. He wasn't on the team, but he was still in.

So on Monday I followed him and got on the same bus.

"Whas up?" I said, sitting down in front of him.

"Why you here?" Terrell asked.

"Just, uh, doing something for my mom," I said, feeling stupid.

"Huh," he said and put in his earphones and started playing on his phone.

Crap.

But when the bus stopped by an elementary school, Terrell's little sister got on.

"Da'Quan!" she squealed and bounced into the seat with me. "You coming over to our house?"

Terrell rolled his eyes and pushed her in the back of the head. "Shut up, Diamond."

They started bickering just like my cousins do. Thinking about my cousins gave me an idea. Nobody had the dirt on everybody like my younger girl cousins. I bet Terrell's sister knew him better than anyone. And as I looked at her, I knew the perfect place to talk.

Breaking into their fighting, I said to Diamond, "Your hair still, uh—"

She nodded hard. "Yeah, why else am I wearing this scarf on my head all the time? My mom says my hair's fiiiiiiine and she don't have time to take me to get it fixed right now or maybe my aunty can do something with it next time she come over—"

"I can take you right now," I interrupted.

"The place my mom goes, Shirley's, it's right around here."

Diamond screamed and tried to hug on me.

"You got your money?" I asked.

"It's in my sock," she said, proudly.

Terrell tried to tell her she couldn't go. But then she said she'd tell their mom that he went over to Iesha's after school sometimes and left her home alone.

"I'll make sure she's okay," I said. "I had to drop something off there anyway. I can just do some homework and then bring Diamond home. Shirley ain't got any kids, and she really loves them."

"Man, I don't know what's wrong with you," Terrell grumbled. "But I guess you ain't a kiddie rapist. Give your number so I can check on her. And you be home before Mom," he said to his sister. "And if she's mad about your hair, it's got nothing to do with me. And I ain't going to no salon, but you better tell Mom I was there, got it?"

Diamond didn't even look back when we got off the bus.

"C'mon," I said, leading the way to Shirley's.

chapter fourteen

I barely had to introduce Diamond. Shirley and her were talking a mile a minute almost right away. I pretended to read while I thought about what I wanted to find out. The good thing about little girls is that they just like to talk. They don't ask why you're asking.

Once she had Diamond sitting for a while waiting for something to happen in her hair, Shirley moved on to a new customer. I pulled my chair over by Diamond.

"How come Terrell's not doing football?" I asked.

"He says it's stupid and getting hit in the head all the time make you stupid. But really he didn't like sitting on the bench all the time last year."

"He better not say that stuff to Montez. He loves football," I said.

She rolled her eyes. "I hate Montez. He's mean. Not nice like you. Terrell should hang with you."

"So why is Terrell Montez's boy?" I asked.

Diamond scrunched up her face. "He always has been, since they was little. But sometimes I think Terrell's tired of Montez. He spends way more time with Iesha now. I heard Iesha used to go with Montez. Did she?"

"Yeah, beginning of last year but not for a long time," I said. "I think Montez cheated on her, but I don't remember a lot of drama. I don't think she really cared."

"She was probably ready to dump him," Diamond nodded. "I like her; she's nice to me."

I didn't know how to ask the next part, but then Diamond took us there.

"I don't know why Iesha's going with Terrell. She's, like, super pretty and super popular . . ."

"Terrell's popular too. Second only to Montez," I told her. "Do you think it's because he's funny?"

"Huh, yeah, I guess. When Montez or Iesha's over, they're always busting up over something Terrell says. He's really good at sounding just like someone. But it ain't for his smarts. He can barely—"

Then Shirley came over and needed to do something else to Diamond's hair. I sighed. I had forgotten how long this hair stuff could take. I used to spend so much time at Shirley's waiting for my mom. When Shirley was finally done, we needed to hurry before Diamond's mom got home.

On the bus Diamond kept asking annoying stuff like didn't I like her hair and who was my girlfriend. I was trying to think. Finally, I just came out with it.

"What's bad about Terrell?" I asked.

But Diamond didn't get my question. She shook her head. "I know, he ain't so bad. Just mean to me because I'm his little sister. But he does watch out for me sometimes. He always calls me when he's at Iesha's to make sure I'm okay."

Just then I got a text from Terrell.

Gt yr azz hm!

"See?" she sighed. "He do care."

"Naw, I meant—"

Diamond stood up and yanked the cord for the bus to stop.

"Thanks, Da'Quan. You're my favorite forever. I'll see you around." She tried to do some weird handshake with me, then jumped off the bus.

chapter fifteen

I watched Terrell for the next few days. The class we had together would have been pretty boring without him. He always had something funny to say at school. Even the teacher had to laugh sometimes at his excuses for not doing his work. And definitely the girls enjoyed him even when they pretended to be mad.

So I decided to go for it. I needed something to help me talk to Ashantay. Terrell had something to say to everybody. And I thought now that I understood this channeling thing better, I could control anything bad that came along with being funny. Maybe the bad thing was that Terrell could be mean sometimes, making fun of people. I'd be careful not to do that too much.

When I was ready, I made sure to sit near him in class. While we were going around taking turns reading aloud, I closed my eyes to do my thing. It took longer than I thought. Terrell was maybe more complicated than I had given him credit for.

But when I opened my eyes again, I started grinning. This junk the girl in front of me was reading was full of the funniest stuff ever. It was about farms or something, but words were jumping out at me: *rod, wood, come, tool.* I couldn't wait for my turn to read because I knew just how I was going to say words like that to crack everyone up.

The teacher called on me, and I looked down at my book. But I couldn't read anything. It was worse than it had ever been for me. It was almost like in my dreams, except instead of moving, all the letters looked like some crazy alphabet from another language.

But even as I was panicking, I said, totally cool, "Aww, man, I can't read this X-rated stuff to these kids. It's like porn."

Everybody busted up. The bell rang. The teacher told me to stay after class. I got after-school detention. Then I went to lunch.

At lunch I tried to ignore the posters and stuff because everything still looked so wrong. Instead, I concentrated on Ashantay. It was easy to talk to her once I knew I could turn anything into a joke and she'd think it was funny.

"Oh my God, Da'Quan," she said, falling into Shaquetta, "I swear I'm gonna pee my pants. Stop!"

Terrell wasn't in lunch, and Montez was busy trying to talk to Layla, this new girl. But everyone else at the table started listening and laughing. It was a great feeling.

When the bell rang, I walked with Ashantay and Shaquetta to their gym class. I was pretending to be Shaquetta and saying what was wrong with everyone's clothes. The girls were screaming with laughter.

"How you do that?" Shaquetta said, wiping

her eyes. "It's like you're inside my head. Except everything you said is totally wrong because you have no fashion sense. That's why I got to share my knowledge, my gift with the world."

She tried to look all serious, but Ashantay pushed her into the wall, giggling.

The bell rang. "Y'all made me late to class, and now I gotta run," I said, running like a fool to make them laugh more.

"Don't you think Da'Quan's cute?" I heard Ashantay say. I thought my smile would split my face. I felt so light as I was running to class that I got there before the teacher closed the door.

chapter sixteen

When I was coming out of detention, I thought I heard cheerleading practice outside. I didn't feel weird at all like I usually would going to watch Ashantay and them. I thought they'd like it.

As I walked up to the cheerleaders, Iesha was looking mad because girls weren't listening or something. When she saw me, she said, "Oh, no. No guys. No distractions. These ladies are having a hard enough time focusing today. We're going to look like crap at the game."

"I promise, I'll be good," I said all wide-eyed.

Ashantay started giggling and nudged Shaquetta. Iesha gave them a dirty look.

"Go sit at that table over there," she ordered me. "Okay, y'all, now I'm serious—"

I sat and got out some homework, but I was really watching the girls. It was all short shorts and tank tops and jumping around. Every time Ashantay snuck a look at me, I waved at her and she got a little smile.

When they finished, I strolled over. Ashantay was all sweaty. She was so hot.

"You going home now?" I asked.

"I was going to take a shower and change," she said, waving to her girls to go ahead without her.

"Naw, you're fine," I said, and she could tell I meant it in all ways.

She blushed. "I'm all gross—"

"C'mon," I said, grabbing her hand and pulling her toward the bus stop. "Which bus you take?"

She pulled away but let her fingers slide through mine. My whole body felt like it was on fire. "Why, you coming over to my house or something?" she said pretending to be mad.

"Naw, I was just going to be nice and ride home with you. Keep all the annoying guys off you, you know? But if you don't want me to . . ."

She pretended to think about it. "Guess I can't stop you. It's a free country." She gave me another little smile.

On the bus I had her laughing all the time, except now it was me she was falling into, not Shaquetta. I was glad I was sitting down so I could hide my tent pole.

"Well, next stop's mine," Ashantay said. "Just in case you got anything to say before I need to get off."

I felt myself turn red, but I didn't hesitate. "Okay, want to go with me to the homecoming dance?"

Now Ashantay was standing up, looking down at me. That was a great view too. She smiled slowly with those beautiful lips. "Okay. But homecoming's not for a while. How about something before then?"

"Uh, yeah, yeah. Uh—" I was so excited, I couldn't talk.

She laughed and patted me on the cheek. "I'll see you tomorrow, and we'll work it out. Bye . . ."

I knew she could feel how hard I was staring at her butt as she walked off the bus. She gave me a little wave before she walked away.

I was so high from her that I rode the bus for a long time before I realized how far from home I was getting. Then my mind couldn't think about anything except Ashantay, so I walked home instead of figuring out a bus. Man, she was good.

chapter seventeen

Class was a little rough the next day. I hadn't done any homework because I was way too distracted. When it was time for lunch, I was so nervous that I almost thought about not going. I was sweating everywhere.

When I sat down, Ashantay was rolling her eyes at Terrell and Montez cracking up about something. She gave me a big smile.

"Hey," I said and stuffed some burrito in my mouth. I didn't know what to say to her. After a couple of tries to talk to me and me just nodding or shrugging, Ashantay started talking to Shaquetta. My stomach tightened up.

When Ashantay got up to get something, Shaquetta hissed at me. "Why you messing with my girl? Yesterday you were all over her like flies on doo-doo, and now today, you're ignoring her? What's wrong with you?"

"I'm not!" I said, surprised. "I just, I don't know—"

Ashantay gave me a look when she came back. I heard Terrell's voice and Montez laughing.

Oh, I thought. *I lost it. I need more Terrell, and then I won't be sitting here like a fool.* I took a deep breath and closed my eyes. I wondered if I could take extra from Terrell.

When I opened my eyes, Ashantay was looking at me. "What are you doing?" she said.

"Thinking about you, baby," I said. "Until right now your beauty freaked me out so much I couldn't talk. But if I just close my eyes, it shouldn't be a problem." I closed my eyes again. "But maybe you should let me touch you so I know where you are."

"Oh my God," Shaquetta snorted.

I felt someone sit down next to me.

"I'm right here," Ashantay said.

I stuck out my hand and hit her arm. Ashantay and Shaquetta screamed. Ashantay grabbed my hand and pulled it up to her face. Keeping my eyes closed, I put my hand on her cheek gently.

"Oh no," I whispered. "It's happening again. I'm getting speechless just feeling your beauty even when I can't see it."

Ashantay sighed. I could almost feel her melt.

"Oh God," Shaquetta said. "Get a room."

I felt Ashantay's cheek move as she smiled.

chapter eighteen

We hung out after school and made plans for the weekend. Then at home I kept texting her, even during dinner.

"Does this girl explain why you're missing assignments?" Mom said. "I checked on the computer and saw you hadn't turned in some homework. This isn't how I wanted you to start the school year, Da'Quan. I'm glad you have a girlfriend. I don't want to put you on restriction, but I will if you aren't doing your homework."

"Dang, Mom," I started to whine, but then I knew a better way. "I do solemnly swear," I said raising my right hand, "to do my—"

"Okay, okay," my mom said, smiling. "I know you can do it if you try. Let me know if you need help."

So after dinner I did crack the books. But every time I tried to read, it was just like before. I could barely recognize the letters. I tried going slow and using a ruler like Ms. White taught me in elementary school, but it was like my eyes couldn't even stay on the words.

I cussed and threw the book.

"What's wrong?" Mom called from the other room.

"Nothing," I said. I stared at my books. I had a lot of reading to do to catch up. I didn't know how I was going to do it now.

I went out to find Mom. "Could you just read some of this to me?" I asked.

She looked worried. "Are you having trouble with reading again, baby? I thought that was so much better for you now."

"Naw, naw, I'm just tired. Please, just a little,

Mom, so I can fill out this worksheet?"

She gave me a look but took my textbook. I tried to focus enough to get the answers to the questions. Writing them down was hard too. My handwriting looked different.

Lying in bed, I admitted that the reading and writing problem must be from Terrell. Man, that sucked for him. I guess that was why he was always cutting up in class.

But I couldn't stop channeling him now. I needed him to keep Ashantay and get in. Already more people were talking to me than before. And it was only a few weeks until homecoming. Later, I could stop with him, but for now, if he could go to school without being able to read, so could I.

chapter nineteen

Life with Ashantay was great. After school we had a spot where we'd go and make out. It was hard to keep my hands off her during school. And I loved the sexy looks she gave me when she knew I was wanting her so bad.

Lunch was the best part of the day now and not just because of Ashantay. I was cracking everybody up all the time. And the good thing was that Terrell didn't seem to mind too much. It was like we knew how to work together to build and build the joke until everyone at our table was snorting soda out of their noses.

One time we were going on Montez, making fun of him, but he was loving it. He always loved being the center of attention. I felt like we were two strippers, trying to top each other, getting him more and more excited. It felt weird.

Afterward, Terrell said to me, "Thursdays, there's open mike for stand up for under eighteen at this place. Maybe you should come."

I thought that was really nice of him. "Thanks, man," I said. "But that was all you, really." I gave him a big smile.

But class was harder and harder. I hadn't turned in anything. I knew it wouldn't be long before Mom checked my grades again online or a teacher called her. Every day I thought maybe I was ready to stop channeling Terrell, but then I couldn't do it.

I needed to talk to someone so I texted Shaun. He said to meet him at the radio station, and he'd give me my tour.

He was right that it was small, but it was cool meeting some of the people whose voices

I'd heard. And they thought I was hilarious.

Then Shaun pulled me outside the door of the room where they were on the air.

"Got a surprise," he said, handing me a piece of paper. "You can read the 'Events This Week' part—oh, there's Reggie waving, go in."

Well, you already know it was a disaster. Reggie was getting pissed that Shaun and me were arguing in whispers in the room while he was on the air. He was trying to fill time, waiting for me to sit down at the microphone. Finally, he just grabbed the paper from me and ran through it fast before going to a commercial break.

"What was that about?" he demanded, glaring at us.

"My fault," Shaun said. "I should have asked him first. You know, some people are scared of public speaking and stuff."

I just looked at my shoes. *I can't keep doing this*, I thought.

So while Shaun was driving me home, I told him everything.

"I know it sounds crazy," I said. "It is crazy.

But it works too. And I don't know what to do next."

"Yeah, it sounds crazy," Shaun said. "And I think it's probably all in your head. You want to get better at something—basketball, talking to girls, whatever. Then you think you got some special power so you believe in yourself and, presto, you get better."

"But what about the bad stuff?" I demanded. "'Cause you know usually I *can* read and junk."

"Maybe it's all just darkness that's already within you that you can't claim as part of yourself. So you have to pretend it's from someone else," Shaun said.

"Man, you talk some stupid mumble jumble, you know that?" I said. "You sound like that guy on *Oprah*."

Shaun just laughed.

"Well, even if you're taking special powers from someone, little cuz, I think you can stop. You got your girl. You don't need smooth talking to keep her. I bet there isn't so much talking going on anyway, hmmm? Am I right? Maybe you want to channel some of my moves with the ladies, you know what I'm saying?" He cackled. Then he got serious.

"But really, Da'Quan, the best part of getting older is just getting better at being yourself and not caring what other people think. The good ones will like you better when you're honest about who you are."

"Yeah, okay, whatever," I muttered.

chapter twenty

But I thought about what Shaun said. Things were pretty comfortable with Ashantay. I still liked to make her laugh, but she liked talking about serious stuff too. She was worried about Shaquetta and Daniel. She wanted to talk about our families. She even wanted to do homework together, and that was hard when I couldn't read.

So I stopped channeling Terrell. It was hard at first not knowing how to put myself in the conversation at lunch anytime I wanted. But I didn't feel so scared of Montez or that I'd say something stupid to everyone now. I felt comfortable with them too. No one had asked me to Iesha's homecoming party yet, but I knew Ashantay thought we were going.

Then Mom had to ruin it all during homecoming week.

"We need to talk," she said after dinner as I started toward my room to text Ashantay and catch up on homework. I didn't have everything in yet, but Ashantay was helping me.

"I swear, Mom," I said. "I'm getting caught up. I'll show you my homework tonight after I do it."

"We'll talk about that in a minute," Mom said, looking tired. "There's something else first. Sit down."

My heart started beating faster.

"You know it's my turn for the susu money soon and I said we'd go somewhere."

I nodded.

"But I've been thinking... How do you think Michelle talks to her kids about Barack using drugs?" Mom said.

I rolled my eyes. My mom has a serious obsession with the Obamas.

"Are you trying to tell me you smoke crack?" I asked.

"Don't you be getting smart," she said. "I never touched that junk. I just wish I had more help talking about hard stuff with you."

"I know about the birds and the bees, Mom," I said. "We had *that* talk."

"Quit interrupting with your nonsense. Do you want to go to Chicago and see your father?"

The question hung in the air. I felt like I couldn't breathe.

"What?" I whispered. "How—"

"I found out a while ago he was back in Chicago. And he let me know through a friend that he'd like to see you if you want to see him," she said flatly.

"Back? Back from—"

"Prison," Mom said, watching me.

"Why—"

"Look, I didn't know for sure where he was. I heard some rumors, but you didn't need that in your life. But now I think you're old enough to start making some choices. I can't—" She kind of broke down.

I didn't even realize I was crying until she put her hand on my cheek.

"You think about it, baby. Shaun said he'd come with us. We could visit my Aunty Betty. But if you don't want to, I understand—"

I shoved away from the table and stood up, shaking.

"I gotta go. I gotta go out," I said, turning for the door.

"Quan, you've still got homework—"

I slammed the door on her words.

chapter twenty-one

You want to know the story on my dad? By the time I was born, my dad was already out of the picture. My mom always said that she didn't know where he was and that she wasn't looking too hard to find him.

"Oh, he's not a bad person," she always said. "But I think you and me, we're just fine the way we are. Don't you think, baby?"

And I did. Lots of kids don't have dads around. And I have a good mom, good family. I never missed him. Hardly ever wondered. And now this.

I found myself at the park. I grabbed an old ball someone had left and started shooting baskets. The more I missed, the madder I got.

My mind was full of questions, each one making me feel worse. What if I met him and he didn't like me? Who was he to like me or not? He didn't even know me. What if Mom came with and he said something bad to her? Would I fight him? What had he been in prison for?

I really did have things inside me from *this* person, my dad. And it wasn't stuff I could stop, like the channeling. What if whatever got him in prison was inside me too? Maybe all the darkness Shaun was talking about was from my dad.

"Aw, man, who taught you to shoot?" a voice in the darkness said. "Ain't you got no daddy or someone to teach you how to be a man?" Montez strolled onto the court, laughing.

He was still laughing when I shoved the ball in his gut and then punched him in the face. In a smooth move, Montez hooked an arm around my neck, like we were buddies, and punched me in the stomach.

"It's good to see you mad, Da'Quan," he hissed in my ear. "You almost never get mad, like a man should. But too bad for you, there's no one here this time to stop this fight. So you're about to find out why I'm the man on top. Because no one can get mad like I can."

As he started to beat on me, I knew not only what I needed to do, but what I wanted so bad. I opened myself up and let Montez's rage flow through me. Then I felt no fear.

Montez loved fighting, and now so did I. I don't know how long we were going at each other. Both our faces were bleeding.

"Get out of here. I'm calling the cops," a lady screamed out her window. I had Montez down on the ground, but I couldn't hold him and punch him. And I knew he'd never give up, so I could never go home. I'd have to hold him forever. But then I saw the lights of the cruiser.

I let go, and Montez sprang up. He leaned in, dripping blood. "I got a record, so I can't stick around now, but this ain't over." Then he spat some blood at me and took off. I was frozen, but as the cops got nearer, I took off running too.

chapter twenty-two

Of course I got put on restriction for running out, fighting, and still not having my grades up. But I didn't even care.

"Whatever—" and then I had to stop myself from cussing at my mom. I've never cussed at her. Cussed about things but never called her a cuss name. Anger at her and everyone in the world was so strong in me that I don't know how I stopped myself. I had to get away.

I went in my room and shut the door in her

face. When she yelled at me through the door, I screamed back, "Leave me alone!"

Silence and then she walked away. I waited until I thought she'd gone to bed to go shower and clean off all the blood.

I couldn't think. I couldn't do anything. I was still shaking. I had texts from Ashantay, but I couldn't deal with her now. Why was she always wanting stuff from me?

I barely slept. Sometimes I had to get up and walk around my room, punching my fist.

Mom left early for work. When I came out to grab something before school, there was a note: *We will talk later.*

I grabbed a pen and wrote **F U** on it as hard as I could and threw it back on the table.

At school all I wanted was to find Montez. I didn't want to see Ashantay. She'd just freak out over my face and want to know how I felt. I didn't have time for that. I waited at Montez's locker, but he never showed. Maybe he wasn't in school.

I was surprised when I saw him in the lunch-room. He broke into a huge grin when he saw me.

"Hey, it's my twin," he said, pointing at his face and mine. I was so confused. I was ready to go outside right now and finish this thing. I stood up.

"Let's go," I said.

"Naw, naw," he waved me down. "Maybe later, man." He leaned over. "I got to keep chatting Layla—I'm gonna get in her pants this weekend. It's another thing men do." He slapped me on the back. I was gritting my teeth so hard, I thought my jaw would break.

Ashantay came hurrying over. "Oh my God, Quan, what happened—I heard—" she looked at Montez.

"Not now," I said, barely opening my lips. "Just leave it."

She glared at me. "Why haven't you answered my texts, Quan?"

Montez laughed, slapping my knee this time. "Sorry, honey, you know how it is. Bros before—well, anyway, me and my man gotta talk; so do you mind?"

Ashantay looked at me, her mouth open. Then she grabbed her stuff and walked off.

"Girls," Montez sighed. "If I didn't like getting laid, I don't think I'd bother."

I felt hot and icy cold at the same time. "How can you—" I didn't know how to say it. "How do you do it?" I whispered. "How do you feel this way all the time?"

"It's tight, ain't it?" Montez said, shoving chicken fingers in his mouth. "You don't never feel weak, that's for sure. Hey, that was a good fight. Too bad the cops came. You didn't get caught, did you?"

I just shook my head and got up. I felt like a monster. I couldn't be around people. So I went home.

chapter twenty-three

By the time Mom came home, I was getting better. I could feel the rage fading, like the volume being turned down. But I still needed to be alone.

I met her at the door.

"I have some things to say, and then I need some time to myself. We can talk later. I skipped school after lunch. I'm sorry, and I'm sorry about last night. Okay?"

"Oh, baby," Mom put her arms out.

"But I want to be alone," I said, going to my

room. She looked so sad, but I couldn't help it.

I tried to focus on homework. Finally, I sent Ashantay a text.

sorry can we talk tomorrow?

She didn't respond.

In the morning I felt like myself again. It felt so good that I was even singing in the shower.

When I got to school, people were walking around in pajamas for Homecoming Week. Some of the girls were carrying teddy bears. Some teachers were wearing bathrobes, which was just weird.

I waited at Ashantay's locker. I saw her coming down the hall. She was wearing bunny slippers, silky shorts, and a tank top so thin, I could see her bra. Mmm.

"You look . . . nice," I said.

"You too good to show some school spirit?" she snapped.

"Naw, I just forgot. Besides, I just sleep in boxers," I said.

"TMI." She wouldn't look at me.

"Ashantay," I said. "I'm really sorry about yesterday. I, I wasn't myself. I was having such a bad day and a bad night. I got in a fight with Montez."

"Yeah, I heard," she said tightly. "Why?"

"Because I was angry because my mom told me my dad's been in prison and now he's out and he wants to see me."

She exhaled and leaned against her locker. "Whoa."

"Yeah."

"You seen him before?"

"Nope."

"Wow." She reached down and took my hand. "I'm glad you're yourself again. I missed you. I cried all last night."

I pulled her close, and she wrapped her arms around my neck. We could have stayed kissing forever.

Then Iesha said, "Hey, lovebirds, you gonna come to my party Saturday after the dance, right?"

We broke apart to say sure and smile at each other. I knew then I didn't need channeling or any other superpower to be happy. I liked what I had right now.

chapter twenty-four

I was done with channeling—I had sworn it. And I didn't mean for anything to happen. I'm still not sure if anything did. All I know is that I think I was different afterward.

After school Ashantay said I could come over to her house. She said her mom was going to be gone for a while.

Ashantay and I were just lying on the couch, holding each other. I know guys are always saying that they just want to get it on and it's girls that want the cuddling and junk. But here's the secret—sometimes guys like that too.

I felt so close to her, but I wanted to get closer. And now I knew how. I thought I could just tune in to her but take nothing.

I should have been nervous after what I'd experienced with other people. But she had me so relaxed. I knew Ashantay wasn't perfect, but she seemed so good. So I closed my eyes and I tuned in.

If you've been paying attention, you won't be surprised to hear that the Ashantay station was nice.

But I think something did happen. I think something slid over to me. Some of that think-more-about-other-people-and-less-about-your-self thing Ashantay had going on. At least that's how I explain what happened at homecoming.

chapter twenty-five

I know at some schools the homecoming dance is a really big deal. At my school we dress up, but it's not like prom or anything. Ashantay wore this short little red dress, and I wore my only tie with jeans. My mom had agreed to let me off restriction for homecoming after I begged her.

But even though homecoming's not as big as prom, it's still not where you want to get dumped. Which is what Shaquetta did to Daniel.

Ashantay said Shaquetta was a little too

excited about Montez's clothes, but she was just interested in them as a fashion statement. I recognized what he was wearing—it was from the same store I got my stuff for the first day of school. I wasn't surprised Shaquetta liked it, but I'm not sure the clothes explained why she was grinding with Montez.

Ashantay said it was because Daniel over-reacted and got really jealous about the clothes thing. Well, he really got mad about the grind-ing and then they were yelling at each other and Shaquetta screamed, "It's over! I can't take it anymore!" Shaquetta ran out the gym door with Ashantay behind her. Daniel punched the wall.

"C'mon, man," I said. "Let's get out of here." Everyone was talking and staring. Daniel kicked the gym door open, and I followed him.

Outside in the darkness, words just poured out of Daniel. None of it was very surprising to me. How he always felt like he had to prove himself, especially to Shaquetta. She was always telling him what was wrong with him and mak-ing him feel worse about himself. Except when she was making him feel great. And now what would he do without her?

Eventually he ran out of words. I just put my hand on his shoulder. What could I say? If I told him he didn't need to prove himself, would that help?

Daniel's phone rang. He looked at it.

"It's my brother," he said. "I gotta talk to him."

He walked around the corner of the building. I thought I could hear him talking, but maybe he just wanted a minute alone to pull himself together.

I looked over to where the girls were sitting on the picnic table. Ashantay had her arm around Shaquetta. Shaquetta's head was on Ashantay's shoulder.

I leaned back against the wall to chill until Daniel came back. Light spilled on the sidewalk as someone opened the gym door. Montez came out.

"Hey, Da'Quan, man. We're leaving for Iesha's. C'mon."

I squinted at him. He was just a shape against the light.

"Nah, I'm waiting on Daniel. I'll catch you later," I said.

Montez snorted and shook his head. "Daniel's a fool. He was so whipped. But you should come now with me. Iesha said she wanted you there. I think you have a chance with her. Did you hear she's thinking about dumping Terrell?"

"I'm with Ashantay," I said, confused.

"So?" said Montez, coming out of the door. "People are together, and then they're not. Look at Daniel and Shaquetta. Maybe you were with Ashantay today. But tonight you could be with Iesha and that's a step up, you know what I'm saying."

I didn't feel excited or angry or anything. I just hoped Daniel was okay. I knew Montez was wrong. I wasn't going to dump Ashantay for Iesha or cheat on Ashantay. I wasn't even going to that party. I'd been thinking so much about it, but now it wasn't important anymore.

"You go ahead," I said, pushing off the wall. "I'll see you later."

Montez yelled something as he went back inside. I wasn't listening.

I ran into Daniel coming around the corner.

"Hey, you waited. Thanks," he said, looking down.

"What you want to do now?" I asked.

"My brother's at his friend's, hanging and shooting baskets. No girls there."

"Can I come?" I asked. It didn't bother me to ask. If he said yes, no, whatever, I was cool.

Daniel looked relieved and surprised. "I thought you were going to Iesha's party?"

I shrugged. "You seem like you need your men around you. No women right now. Except maybe your mama."

Daniel looked up fast to see if I was making fun of him. I wasn't and he could tell.

"You like your mom?" he asked, looking at the ground again.

"Love her," I said, and it was true.

"Me too," he said. "I mean, mine, not yours. Not that your ma ain't . . ." We both laughed.

I sent Ashantay a text telling her what was up.

I love how you love your friends, she texted back. *That's a gift, Quan.*

chapter twenty-six

After that, I didn't exactly stop caring, but I quit caring so much. Maybe people didn't stand up and yell my name when they saw me, like they did for Montez, but I had friends.

I didn't eat at Montez's table much anymore because Daniel couldn't eat with Shaquetta. Shaquetta said she wasn't going to stop eating lunch where she wanted and she was eating with them. Daniel said he didn't care and that table was too loud anyway.

Ashantay sat with us, and there were always more people who wanted to sit with Montez than there was room for. Some of those extra people ended up with us, and they were better than just extra.

So things were pretty good, now that I'd stopped wanting all the time. Then the dude showed up again, and I wasn't exactly happy to see him.

I dreamed I was at a party and everyone was slapping me on the back and laughing at everything I said. Okay, so maybe I hadn't completely stopped wanting. But in this dream it felt different—I was relaxed and enjoying it, not feeling like it was some amazing impossible thing.

Then everybody turned and looked at the door. And they all had fish heads, which was weird, but whatever, I like fish. At least I like eating them. I looked too to see who was coming.

The dude walked in, wearing Montez's clothes from the homecoming dance. He stopped and looked down at himself and shook his head.

"I am not liking the sartorial sense in your dreams," he said to me.

"Whaaaaat?" I said.

"It means I think these clothes suck," he said.

I laughed. "Yep, they kind of do," I said.

"So how's it going?" he asked. "Is this—" he pointed at everybody (some still had fish heads) "what your life is like for real now that you have the gift?"

That's when I started getting mad.

"You set me up," I said, getting in his face.

"Fight, fight!" everyone started chanting.

"Excuse me?" he said, raising one eyebrow.

"You knew that every time I tried to channel something good from someone, I would get something bad too. And it's all bogus anyway." I folded my arms.

The dude put on the concerned adult look, the one I hate. "You felt like you channeled some of the darkness from others into yourself, Da'Quan?"

I shrugged and mumbled, "Whatever. Basically it's just BS, everything you said."

The dude smiled to himself. "Well, that's just too bad. I did warn you I wasn't exactly sure about that gift. But how are things with you these days anyway? How's Ashantay?"

I felt my face break into a huge smile. I looked around the room. Wasn't Ashantay here somewhere? I noticed now that some of the fish-head people were swimming around up by the ceiling.

"She's good, really good, if you know what I mean," I laughed.

The dude shook his head. "I know you're a hormonal mess right now, Da'Quan, but is Ashantay really only important to you as a sex object?"

I stared at the ground. It was hard to talk to other guys about how safe Ashantay made me feel, all the stuff I could tell her. Talking to her was helping me figure out what I wanted to do about my dad.

Finally, I said, "She's good. It's good with us. And I didn't mean just like that." I thought the dude would get what I was trying to say.

Just then I saw Ashantay coming through

the crowd. She didn't have a fish head, and she looked beautiful. Not just hot, but like all the caring for other people inside her had spilled out and made her sparkle on the outside. She saw me and called my name, smiling the biggest smile.

"Looks like you're going to be busy," the dude said, winking at me. "It's been nice knowing you. Good luck." He shook my hand, but I barely noticed because I was pushing past people to get to Ashantay.

When I woke up, I kept my eyes closed, trying to hold on to the feeling of having my arms around Ashantay, our bodies pressed together. Finally, it faded, but before I lost it completely, I rolled over and grabbed my phone.

Miss you. Be mine, I texted her. I thought about Ashantay sleeping, my text waiting for her in the morning. I fell back to sleep holding a pillow, hoping I'd dream about her.

About the Author

Elizabeth Karre is a writer and editor. She lives in St. Paul, Minnesota.

what gift would you choose?

the *Gift*

the *Gift*

all you are

elizabeth karre

calling the shots

elizabeth karre

certain signals

elizabeth karre

no regrets

elizabeth karre

IT'S THE OPPORTUNITY OF A LIFETIME— IF YOU CAN HANDLE IT.

Box-Office Smash
D. M. PAIGE

THE OPPORTUNITY

The Campaign
ELIZABETH KARRE

THE OPPORTUNITY

Chart Topper
D.M. PAIGE

THE OPPORTUNITY

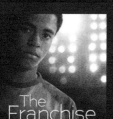

The Franchise
PATRICK JONES with BRENT CHARTIER

THE OPPORTUNITY

Going to Press
D.M. PAIGE

THE OPPORTUNITY

Size 0
D.M. PAIGE

THE OPPORTUNITY

THE OPPORTUNITY